LITTLE MISS LUCKY
and the Naughty Pixies

Roger Hargreaves

Original concept by
Roger Hargreaves

Written and illustrated by
Adam Hargreaves

EGMONT

Little Miss Lucky, as I am sure you know, is the luckiest person in the world.

When she goes out for a walk, she always finds a pound coin lying on the ground.

She never gets caught in the rain.

And even when things go wrong, she is lucky.

The other week she locked herself out of Horseshoe cottage, where she lives, and guess who should come round the corner?

Mr Latchkey the locksmith!

However, last week, strange things started to happen to Little Miss Lucky.

The sort of things that never normally happened to her.

Unlucky things.

She walked under a ladder and a pot of paint fell on her head.

SPLAT!

When she was walking down the high street, she fell into an open manhole.

BUMP!

And as she was passing someone's garden,
she was soaked by a sprinkler.

SPLASH!

Little Miss Lucky could not understand what was going on.

But have you noticed anything? Have you noticed anyone new nearby when these unlucky things happen? That's right, some small troublemakers are playing tricks on her!

And do you know who they are?

I'll tell you.

They are Pixies. Very naughty Pixies!

Poor Little Miss Lucky did not know that Pixies were to blame though. She thought that her luck had run out.

She was so worried that she went to see Doctor Makeyouwell.

But the Doctor was not there. And nobody knew what had happened to him.

"More bad luck," thought Little Miss Lucky to herself.

The next day, she paid another visit to Doctor Makeyouwell's surgery.

But, again, he was not there.

Double bad luck!

On her way home, Little Miss Lucky met Little Miss Wise and explained to her how she had run out of luck.

"I suspect," suggested Little Miss Wise, "that it is not so much a case of bad luck, as somebody playing tricks on you. Somebody like Mr Mischief, for instance."

The more Little Miss Lucky thought this over, the more she hoped that Little Miss Wise was right.

That evening she devised a plan to catch the culprit.

She sprinkled flour on the floor round her bed before she went to sleep.

In the middle of the night, while Little Miss Lucky was fast asleep, those naughty Pixies crept into her house.

Their first naughty deed was to swap the sugar in the sugar bowl with the salt in the salt-cellar.

Then the Pixies sneaked upstairs and left the largest alarm clock you have ever seen on Little Miss Lucky's bedside table.

Very early the next morning, Little Miss Lucky was rudely awoken by the most awful noise.

CLANG! CLANG! CLANG! rang the giant alarm clock.

Little Miss Lucky's ears were ringing.

When she looked down at the floor, there was a trail of floury footprints for her to follow out of the door and down the stairs.

Floury footprints that were much too small to be Mr Mischief's.

And, as I am sure you can guess, those floury footprints led Little Miss Lucky all the way to where the Pixies lived.

The Pixies were so surprised and worried at being caught that they promised there and then to never play another trick on Little Miss Lucky.

Little Miss Lucky left feeling very happy knowing that she was just as lucky as she had always been.

When she got home, she made herself a well earned breakfast. Eggs on toast and a pot of tea.

She was so busy thinking about the Pixies that, without realising, Little Miss Lucky poured salt in her tea and sugar on her eggs!

But you and I know that she didn't, did she?!

Because of the naughty Pixies' night time tricks, her breakfast was not spoiled.

Now, that's what I call lucky!